FEB 18

TEEN (LW)

The library is always open at
renfrewshirelibraries.co.uk

Visit now for
homework help
and free
eBooks.

SKOOBS

We are the Skoobs and we love the library!

ne: 0300 300 1188
il: libraries@renfrewshire.gov.uk

Smile

The story of the original Mona Lisa

MARY HOFFMAN

Barrington Stoke

First published in 2018 in Great Britain by
Barrington Stoke Ltd
18 Walker Street, Edinburgh, EH3 7LP

www.barringtonstoke.co.uk

Text © 2018 Mary Hoffman

A CIP catalogue record for this book is available
from the British Library upon request

ISBN: 978-1-78112-717-9

Printed in China by Leo

CONTENTS

ONE

The First Born

"Lovely Lisa," he always called me. Of course, I was a baby then so I don't know if I remember his words or if someone told me. But whenever I felt sad about something I hugged the words "lovely Lisa" to comfort me.

I hugged, too, the knowledge that Leonardo, the greatest artist in Italy, drew my portrait when I was little.

I was the first child born to my parents. I know now that my father's first thought was probably, 'A girl? Oh no! I'll have to find a dowry if she's to have a husband.' But in the four golden years before my little brothers and sisters came along, I never felt that Father was disappointed in me.

And his second thought might have been, 'At last – a living child!' Father had lost two wives and the babies in their wombs before his third wife, my mother, made him a father. He loved me the more because of that, I'm sure.

We were not rich, but not poor either. We lived in the magnificent city of Florence – in a rented house in a rather smelly street on the south side of the river. My father insisted that our family was noble in origin and that – as a nobleman – he had no need for a job.

He owned farms outside the city and the money we lived on came from the rents that farmers paid him and the sale of wheat and animals. And as our family grew, with my three brothers and three sisters, the money had to stretch further.

So, what I remember of my early childhood was lots of love, especially from my father, enough food and clothes but nothing grand, a house in stinky old Via Squazza, and the story that a great artist had drawn my picture as a baby.

But I knew it was more than a story because that great artist, Leonardo da Vinci himself, had left my parents one of his drawings. Of course, Leonardo wasn't so well known then. As I got older, I asked my parents about him and found that he had left Florence when I was three to go to work for the Duke of Milan.

And yet I could just remember the young man with the long fair hair and the velvet cloak the colour of roses. He was so very good-looking that I thought he was some kind of angel.

Leonardo was nearly thirty when he drew me for the first time. His father was Piero, a notary in the city, and Leonardo was his only child.

"But born out of wedlock," my mother insisted. She took a strict view on such matters. "It was good of Piero to accept Leonardo as his son, when he was the result of a tumble with a servant."

Even when I was very young and innocent, I felt this wasn't quite right. Piero didn't deserve praise for that. I knew it took two people to make a baby.

And so Piero da Vinci accepted this son, who turned out to be such a remarkable man. Piero and his first wife – for old Piero would go on to have four wives and twelve children – both raised that first boy.

Because he was born out of wedlock, Leonardo couldn't be a lawyer or a doctor or even a notary like his father. And so, when his talent began to show, Leonardo was made apprentice to one of the city's great painters – a man called Andrea with the nickname "of the True Eye".

*

"Lovely Lisa, lovely Lisa," my little brothers and sisters chanted when they wanted to tease me, which was often. They thought I gave myself airs, because a famous man drew me. Just imagine if they had known about when he would do it again!

I did give myself some airs and graces, to be honest. But that's because I was the first born and my father made much of me, even when he had sons later.

As well as that, I soon learned that the family's fortunes depended on me, and that was a heavy burden to bear.

"You will have to marry well," my mother repeated often. By "well" she meant I must marry a man with money. I learned this along with my

Ave Maria and *Pater Noster* soon after I could first walk and talk.

My best friend as I grew up was a girl called Ginevra. She too was from one of the old families who were no longer wealthy and she too had been taught from her early years that she must "marry money". I think we both thought husbands were made of gold and silver until we were older and knew better.

It was clear that our family fortunes were in trouble. There was less meat on the table and more mending for me and Mother to do. I saw the frown my mother sometimes wore become a fixed crease between her eyebrows.

We started moving house, never to anywhere smart. It felt as if we were restless, rootless. For the first time in my life, I felt scared. What if our money troubles got worse? I knew my father's family were too noble for him to have trained for any kind of work.

I didn't have to wonder what my mother thought of that. Her mouth went into a tight, straight line that matched her frown. But she would never complain about my father to me –

she too came from a noble family, so she knew what he expected from life.

The trouble was, Mother had her own expectations, which didn't include living in rented rooms in dark, grimy streets.

It was my grandparents – my mother's parents – who found us somewhere a bit better. We rented a house from a rich widow, and my father was very grateful.

"It's only a few paces away from Ser da Vinci's house," he said.

Leonardo was away in Milan and there was little chance that I would see him again, but the closeness to him made me feel better too.

TWO

Paint and Blood

Of course, Leonardo was not the only artist in
Florence. In fact, when I was little and I saw all
the statues and paintings on the walls in churches
and the cathedral, I believed that artists ruled the
city!

In time, I learned that the painters and
sculptors were looked down on – yet every
nobleman still wanted their art to adorn their
houses and chapels. They treated the artists as
workmen – like masons and bricklayers – and paid
them for their services, one project at a time.

But, maybe because of my tiny link with
Leonardo, I had nothing but respect for all the
city's artists. I was in awe of the bright colours,

the gold leaf, the shapely marble limbs of the statues.

Florence was full of painters' workshops where apprentices learned their trade. They started with small tasks – they swept floors and mixed colours – but some of them went on to be famous painters in their own right.

Leonardo had once been such an apprentice. But now a duke in Milan paid him handsomely for his art.

And I knew another artist, who I thought might do great things one day. His father, Lodovico, was a friend of my father's and he lived with his family of five boys in a street near ours.

Of the five boys, it was Michelangelo – four years older than me – who was the one I liked best. Michelangelo was named after the Archangel Michael. He had a temper that was far from angelic – but he could certainly draw like an angel.

I knew that Lodovico's wife was not Michelangelo's mother, or his brothers'. My mother had told me that their mother, Francesca, had died when her youngest son was just a baby.

"My heart goes out to Lodovico, trying to bring up five boys on his own," Mother told me. "I was glad when he re-married."

The second wife, the boys' step-mother, was called Lucrezia, which was also my mother's name. What a task she had taken on to bring up five sons! And she had no children of her own.

It was no surprise to me when Michelangelo insisted that his father send him to be an apprentice at a famous painter's workshop. I think Michelangelo suffered many beatings before he got his way. But he was one of the most determined people I ever knew.

Michelangelo didn't stay in that workshop for very long before Lorenzo the Magnificent, the chief of the noble de' Medici family, took him into his household to learn sculpture. After that, Michelangelo's fortune was made. He was a dear friend to me and always such an interesting person. Even when he got a broken nose in an argument with another apprentice, I didn't mind!

Lorenzo de' Medici loved art as much as I did. He was a great patron and his *palazzo* in the Via Larga was full of treasures. Just as all Florence was.

Florence was a strange city – full of contrasts. On the one hand, all those wonderful murals and mosaics and sculptures and elegant buildings. On the other, violence always simmered below the surface. All the young men carried knives and many had tempers as hot as Michelangelo's. Fights could break out with no warning.

When I was 13, I saw one young man kill another.

It's the truth. I was walking with my friend Ginevra the summer after my 13th birthday – the summer I became a woman. That July the city sweltered in the heat. It was like living in the bottom of an iron bowl, surrounded by hot coals.

We shouldn't have been out so late on our own, but it was still light and we both felt we would never sleep in our stuffy houses. We had slipped out to get a breath of air.

We were walking along the south bank of the river Arno, but there was no breeze coming off the sluggish water. The air was tense – so close and muggy that I felt my head would explode.

In the square outside Santo Spirito church we heard voices and then saw two groups of young

10

men, pointing and pulling angry faces at one another.

Ginevra pulled at my arm as if to say, "Come away."

But I was drawn to the scene like a moth to a candle. There was a compelling energy in their rage. Two young men were now facing each other and spluttering with anger, their voices loud and the insults flowing.

A fair-haired youth dressed all in black faced up to a shorter, darker one in a red tunic.

We had no idea what their fight was about. Their voices were so loud and their words tumbled out so fast that they might have been speaking a different language. The shouts rose to a crescendo of swear-words, then they started to shove and push at each other.

If they had been a pair of dogs, someone would have thrown a bucket of water over them, but as they were humans, everyone let them be.

And then – horribly, unexpectedly – a blade flashed. The shorter young man fell on the cobbles, as blood spurted from his mouth and stained his tunic a darker red.

In an instant, the square cleared and the dying man was left alone. I'm ashamed to say that Ginevra and I ran away too. We could do nothing to save him.

As we ran back home, thunder rumbled and the rain poured down on us, drenching our clothes and plastering our hair to our heads. We shivered with cold and fear and I imagined the rain washing the blood away from the Piazza Santo Spirito.

The body of a young man would be left there, as soaked as if it had been fished out of the river.

THREE

An Ordinary Girl

I was 15 years old and a hopeless romantic when we moved in with the rich widow. My mother's aim in life was to turn me into a practical young woman fit to be a wife.

"But you were not married till you were 21," I protested.

This was a sore point. At our level of society in Florence – a level I was reminded of every day – it was normal for girls to marry at 15. If they reached 17 without a promise of marriage, they might never marry at all.

In my mother's case, her family had been too fussy. They wanted wealth as well as birth, and she was close to the only other option – to become a nun – when my father's proposal was accepted.

There were times when I thought the life of a nun might have suited my mother better, but then I would never have been born. And my mother was determined that my fate would not be that of a nun.

All I wanted was a husband who wasn't too old and wasn't too hideous. In fact, what I really wanted was a tall man with fair hair and a velvet cloak the colour of roses. I told you, I was a romantic.

One day I made the mistake of telling my mother my dreams. She hit the roof!

"What makes you so special?" Mother demanded. "Why should you have a young, handsome and rich husband, who is also a member of one of the old families? Only a Medici girl can expect that, and even they can't choose their own husband. Remember, you are nothing but an ordinary girl and your face is your fortune!"

'So,' I thought, 'my mother is very cross with me but she still thinks I'm beautiful.'

The Medici were the greatest of all the great families in our city. All the old noble families knew each other, even the poorer ones. So

Ginevra and I knew two of the Medici slightly –
Contessina and Giuliano, who were both a little
older than me.

When I wasn't dreaming about a man in a
velvet cloak, I thought Giuliano might do as a
husband. He was very good-looking and I think
Ginevra dreamed of him too ...

But what my mother said was true. No Medici
could choose who to marry, the boys no more than
the girls.

And Contessina and Giuliano had a great
sadness to deal with. Their father, Lorenzo de'
Medici – known as "the Magnificent" – had died
a year ago and their oldest brother Piero had
become head of the family.

I had met Lorenzo de' Medici a few times at
the family's grand *palazzo* on the Via Larga, when
I went to visit Contessina. I was in awe of such a
famous person, but Lorenzo was always kind to
me. He was very ugly but so very charming.

I think the whole city mourned Lorenzo when
he died and I was sorry for my friends. And what
would happen to Michelangelo now his patron was
dead? I looked at my father, with his bony, noble

face and his old, worn coat, and was so glad I still had him to love me and make me feel special.

But soon my city, which had been so proud of Lorenzo, turned on his son Piero and drove him and his family out of Florence and into exile. That meant an end to my girlish chats with Contessina de' Medici and my flirty looks with Giuliano.

Contessina was to be married – to Piero Ridolfi. And as I too was thrown on to the marriage market, I thought how I couldn't have been born at a worse time.

All was turmoil in the city.

Piero de' Medici, had lasted only two years as the head of his great family – and of Florence itself.

So, who ruled the city now? Officially the Republic, but a new force was at work. Savonarola was a preacher with fire in his belly who had always railed against the Medici family.

Savonarola preached against all kinds of luxury and pleasure. He believed the rich and powerful people of Florence would burn in Hell. I was terrified of him. Just one of his sermons frightened the life out of me.

And I didn't see what his fury had to do with me. There was no luxury in my family home and I longed for the silks and velvets and ribbons and jewels that Savonarola claimed would send a person straight to Hell. Ginevra longed for beauty and romance as much as I did, but she had as little experience of either.

Ginevra had not been drawn by a great artist, but still I thought her beautiful because I could see her lovely character in her face. But my mother said she was plain, with only her family name to recommend her.

So, there we were, both waiting to see who would come to court us and both knowing we would have no say in the matter of who would marry us.

Then, at the end of the year, I learned a new name.

Francesco del Giocondo was a silk merchant and a widower with a small son in need of a mother.

My heart sank. Surely a widower would be old? But I knew my father and Francesco would settle the details between themselves. Whether I liked him or not, I would be the wife of Francesco.

FOUR

An Engagement

I have never been so nervous in my life as the day Francesco first called at our house. I put on my best dress of green silk, but even that had frayed at the cuffs. My mother had stayed up late to sew new lace on them.

I wore my only piece of jewellery – a single strand of pearls left to me by my grandmother. Mother brushed my hair till it shone and it flowed loose around my shoulders.

As I walked into the *salone* of our rented home I could hardly put one foot in front of the other.

My first thought when I saw my future husband was, *Savonarola would send him straight to Hell*.

Francesco was wearing a tunic with gold thread in the sleeves and a fur collar. Jewels gleamed on his fingers. The preacher wouldn't have approved of him at all!

My second thought was that he looked as nervous as I was.

And my third? *Well, at least he's not bald or fat!*

Francesco made a graceful bow as I entered the room, but I could see that his lip trembled and he stumbled a little over his words.

He had brought several rolls of silk as presents for me, my mother and my sisters to have dresses made. I couldn't help but gasp as I saw the reds and greens and blues of the shimmering silks. They were exquisite.

And, just for me, Francesco had a ruby pendant on a gold chain. I had never owned anything so fine.

This Francesco was indeed not bald or fat. He was less than thirty years old and had a full head of dark brown hair. He wasn't handsome but he wasn't ugly either. I breathed a sigh of relief at the sight of his pleasant face.

Our time alone on that first visit was short, as was the custom, but Francesco stayed to eat dinner with us. I could not eat much. I was worried I might spill something or choke on a bit of food and have to be thumped on the back.

As I went to bed that night I knew I would not have an angel-haired artist or a handsome noble for my husband. But I knew too that I would soon lead a comfortable life. I knew I would spend it with a man I could imagine as a friend and, in time, someone I could love.

But the important meetings were not between me and Francesco, but between him and my father.

Francesco del Giocondo's first wife had come with a fine dowry and my family could not match that. But Francesco had his own business interests – a share in his family's silk workshops and in two farms outside Florence. He didn't need a large dowry from my father.

So why did he want to marry me?

I was afraid to ask my parents but I did. Before my father could answer, my mother said, "Because he is a nobody. A merchant with not a drop of noble blood."

"So you consider my husband-to-be a nobody?" I said. "But you are willing to sell me to him?"

My father looked alarmed. It was very rare for a girl to refuse a marriage contract. And when it did happen it could lead to years of vendetta between the two families.

I wasn't going to refuse to marry Francesco. But I wanted my parents to know I had a mind of my own. And I didn't want to feel that the man I was to spend my life with was "a nobody".

My mother tried to smooth down my ruffled feathers.

"Oh Lisa," she said. "Of course we would never sell you! We are making a contract that benefits both sides. You will be the wife of a rich man and he will have a mother for his little boy and his future children will be nobly born too."

For a moment I had forgotten the little boy. I was to become a mother at 15 without the dangers of childbirth. I hoped the boy would like me.

"Far from selling you, Lisa," my father said as he paced up and down. "I have agreed to give Francesco San Silvestro as your dowry."

San Silvestro! It was a farm in the countryside, owned by our family for years. We drank wine made from the red grapes that grew there and cooked with the green-gold oil made from our own olives.

All that would continue in my new home, but I knew what how difficult it must have been for my father to give away San Silvestro. I kissed him and promised to be a good daughter.

The next time I met Francesco was in his house in Via della Stufa. He shared it with his two brothers and their wives and four sisters, his mother and his two-year-old son, Bartolomeo. The house was bursting with the chatter of women and the rustle of their silk dresses. Servants ran to and fro with refreshments, and messages went back and forth to the kitchen.

'Where is the space for me in this busy household?' I thought in despair. 'How can I carve myself a place here?'

Bartolomeo was shy, but his grandmother and aunts pushed the little boy forward to meet me and he said a quiet "Hello".

I saw what I must do. Francesco wanted a mother for his son and that was what I would be.

FIVE

A True Wife

Ginevra was not so lucky. As I was meeting Francesco, she was introduced to her husband-to-be, Bernardo. He had been widowed twice and was nearly forty years old.

Ginevra was no older than me, but she would have a ready-made family of two sons and three daughters.

When I first met her husband-to-be I saw that he had less hair and more flesh on him than Francesco. But Ginevra had already told me that – and at the same time she'd shown me the sapphire and diamond necklace Bernardo had given her. Jewels sparkled on his fingers, too, and he was dressed like the rich banker he was.

But Bernardo was polite and well-spoken and treated my friend with great kindness and respect. I did not envy Ginevra, but I thought she might be happy as a married woman.

It was time for both of us to stop being romantic girls and to accept our duty – to marry rich men and help our less-than-rich families. If our new husbands were kind to us, we could ask for nothing more.

And now I was thrown into my wedding preparations. Like all the girls in Florence I had a *cassone* – a painted marriage chest – which my mother had been filling since I was born. Now it was time to take everything out and see what I still needed.

But thanks to Francesco's generosity, I lacked for nothing. Even my woollen dresses had silk sleeves. I had my fine underwear, shoes and slippers, gloves, stockings, handkerchiefs, ribbons, purses and combs and mirrors, as well as my work basket and my writing stand with inkstand and pens.

How Savonarola would have hated everything in my *cassone*! I had heard a rumour that the fiery preacher planned to build a huge bonfire in the Piazza della Signoria and force noble men and women to throw their precious luxuries into the flames!

But my most precious thing, between two sheets of paper at the bottom of my *cassone*, was Leonardo's drawing of me as a baby. My mother had given it to me to take to my new home. I shuddered at how fast a bonfire's flames would turn the drawing to ashes and vowed never to let Savonarola get his hands on it.

The final item was a doll of Santa Margherita, in a fine brocade dress. Every bride had one, as a fertility charm, and I knew Ginevra would have one too. I wondered how many children we would both have. Ginevra already had five step-children to look after, but there would be plenty of help in her new home, even if she had five more of her own.

I shivered in the winter air that whistled through the cracks in our rented house. I wasn't afraid of what I must do to make babies – my mother had explained it to me – but I was afraid to give birth. I knew of so many women who had died in childbirth, including my father's two first wives.

I shook my head to get that image out of my mind and looked instead at the gifts Francesco had sent. I had never seen so many jewels or so much gold.

My parents were determined that I should have a wedding dress and head-dress worthy of all the gifts Francesco had given me. I had chosen a crimson velvet over-gown. It was embroidered with pomegranates – a fruit to symbolise fertility – and had sleeves decorated with gold and silver thread. My head-dress was made of pearls.

All this finery marked the big change in my life that was about to take place. I would leave my parents' home and become mistress of Francesco's home – a household that was full of women older than me. I must leave girlish, romantic ideas behind and behave with dignity and grace.

The day came for our exchange of vows.

The notary came to my parents' house, together with all our family and friends.

I was so nervous, I don't know how I managed to walk into the room in my heavy, embroidered dress. But I heard a little gasp from the guests and that gave me courage. I don't know whether they were impressed by my wedding finery or by my looks. But Francesco gazed at me as if I was truly special. And he seemed almost handsome that day, with his pleasant face close shaven and smiling.

The notary asked our names and ages. Francesco was nearly twice as old as me, but that was nothing unusual. Then we had to say that we consented freely to this union. Then came the vows to love and honour each other and, in my case, to obey and serve my husband.

Francesco put a ring on my finger and that was it – we were man and wife.

Everyone cheered and clapped and soon they were all drinking to our health and congratulating us. I felt dizzy with relief. Nothing had gone wrong and I had done my parents proud.

Ginevra came up to us, along with Bernardo. They would be married in the same ceremony as us in a few weeks.

"How beautiful you look, Lisa!" Ginevra said. She put her arm around me and kissed me on both cheeks, while Bernardo and Francesco clasped hands.

'*Lovely Lisa*,' I thought. How I wished that Leonardo could see me today. What a portrait he could paint of me in my wedding dress!

Two days later my husband and I dressed again in our finery and went to the church of Santa Croce for our wedding to be blessed. Now all that was left was the day on which I would go in procession from my parents' house to Francesco's much grander house on the Via della Stufa.

Then my true life as a wife would begin.

SIX

Queen for a Day

The procession to Francesco's home marked the most important step. My wedding would not be complete until I had spent my first night in my husband's bed.

It was a fine, sunny day when I left my family's home to set out on the most significant walk of my life. I was arm-in-arm with my new husband, both of us dressed again in our wedding finery.

My family walked with us – my little sisters and brothers, distant cousins and in-laws – and all our friends. Francesco's family waited at his house to welcome me as his new bride.

In the streets passers-by cheered and musicians played recorders and drums to accompany our procession. Everyone threw flowers and sang to us. People leaned out of their windows and waved and shouted congratulations.

Everyone in Florence loved a good wedding and the bride's procession to the groom's house was something they could all join in with. And everyone knew everyone else – at least by sight. So I heard people call out, "Lisa and Francesco" at every step. And there were even shouts of "Lovely Lisa!", which reminded me of Leonardo. If only he could have seen me all grown up on this walk to my husband's house!

Just as my mother and aunts had promised, I felt like a queen for this one special day.

The procession wound its way along the Via Ghibellina and past the Bargello – the prison, which I prayed my life would have nothing to do with. Children ran along beside us and shopkeepers called out their good wishes.

Then we were at the great bulk of the Duomo, our city's famous cathedral. We made our way past the Duomo's pink, white and green marble walls, as they shone in the spring sunshine like the icing on a wedding cake. Then around the side of the tall and elegant bell tower, designed by the great Tuscan artist Giotto, 150 years ago.

Santa Croce was "our" church, the one where I and all my family worshipped, but all the people of Florence had a special affection for the Duomo. Its massive dome could be seen from every point in the city.

At the west end stood the older black and white Baptistery, where I, just like all Florentine citizens, had been baptised. Francesco looked at me and smiled. I knew he was wondering how soon we'd have a baby to baptise there and how many babies we'd have over the years of our marriage. I blushed at the thought.

We were now in the grand Piazza del Duomo in front of the cathedral's rough west face. A crowd thronged around us to wish us luck.

I had a sudden panic that the mad preacher Savonarola might see me in my velvet gown and scream at me for my sinful luxury. But there was no sign of his black robes and hooked nose.

We went on up the Via Larga and past the *palazzo* where the Medici had lived. I wondered what Contessina was doing now. I knew that if the Medici hadn't been exiled she would have taken part in my procession, and perhaps her handsome brother Giuliano too.

We seemed to have been walking for hours, but in truth it was only a short way to the Via della Stufa where my new life in Francesco's comfortable home awaited me.

At last we arrived and we went in to the sound of cheers. So many people were waiting to receive me – not just Francesco's large family! Everyone who could always came to a wedding feast, where they were sure of a warm welcome and a wonderful meal.

There were so many greetings and good wishes to accept that I was soon weary, but I still had hours to go. The house was full of guests, musicians and jugglers. I had no chance of a few minutes on my own – I was the bride and all eyes were on me.

But at last the end of festivities came. My mother placed a baby boy in my arms to wish me lots of sons in the future and slipped a gold coin into my shoe, for wealth.

I was glad to hand the baby back to his mother, because he looked as if he was about to cry. And I slipped the coin back to my mother. I knew how few coins she had to spare.

My mother had often been sharp with me, but I wouldn't have been human if I hadn't shed a few tears when she left to go back with my father and my brothers and sisters to the only home I had ever known. Oh, it might have been in different rented houses in the city's darker corners, but "home" had always meant my noisy, messy, unruly family.

But I didn't have long to feel sad. Francesco's family were waiting to escort us to our bedroom. By tomorrow morning I would be a married woman indeed.

SEVEN

Meo and Me

Of what passed between me and my new husband
that night, I shall stay silent. But I had no reason
to think differently of him from how I had before –
he was a kind man, whom I could come to love
in time. And he seemed happy with me, giving
me a gold ring to go with my wedding ring. This
one was set with a large diamond, as a symbol of
harmony between man and wife. I hoped it would
prove true of us.

My new sisters-in-law, who were so much
older than my real sisters, fed me a breakfast
of fresh eggs and meat, and petted me like the
youngest child of the house. Which I was, apart
from little Bartolomeo, who came to sit next to
me.

It was a new experience for me. I was used to being the oldest child – the firstborn, who must set a good example to the younger ones.

After Francesco's present, it was a morning of rings! All the married del Giocondo women clustered around me with gifts of rings. It was one of our traditions – brides were given rings to wear for a few years and then they'd give them to other new brides in turn. My wedding ring and the ring with the diamond were the only ones I would keep for ever.

Later that afternoon my father called on me.

"I have come from the notary's," he said, after kissing me and admiring the parlour in which I sat. "I have just signed San Silvestro over to Francesco."

I knew how Father loved that farm and my heart filled with gratitude. I rang a little bell and asked a servant to bring wine and pastries for my guest.

My guest! I had never been able to do anything for my father – except love and honour him – and here I was, the mistress of my own house at 15, calling for refreshments and asking him to sit in a comfortable chair.

I noticed Father had put on his wedding clothes for this important day and I was glad not to see him looking shabby.

"I shall tell my husband," I said, as I blushed at the unfamiliar word.

"You will be happy, won't you, Lisa?" my father asked. He took both my hands in his. "I know you will be comfortable and I think you will be treated well, but I want you to be happy too."

"I shall be happy, Papa," I said. "I have decided to be happy."

And I had.

*

After all, I had a lot to be happy about. Instead of sleeping on a thin mat with my sisters I now lay every night in a high wooden bed on cotton sheets over a thick mattress and under a goose feather quilt. I had never slept in such comfort before.

There was plenty of food and good wine at every meal and I could call for tasty snacks any time I wanted.

I now had many items of clothing in my marriage chest, from silk and cotton under-blouses to day dresses of the finest wool and grand gowns of brocade and velvet. I would open the chest and stare inside at the beautiful things, running my hands over the softness and luxury.

And those hands were covered in rings of gold and jewels from the first days of my marriage.

But best of all, I had no chores to do! There were far too many servants and older women in the house for that. No sewing or mending, no preparing meals or sweeping rooms, no trips to the market. At first I thought it was wonderful just to think about my good luck. I would look at my fine new home and breathe in the fresh scents of herbs in the main rooms or the aroma of cinnamon and cloves from the kitchen.

But after the first few weeks of visits from other married women – almost all older than me – or visits to others, I began to feel bored.

So I decided to focus on my little step-son, Bartolomeo. Everyone called him "Meo", which suited him. It was close to "mio" meaning "mine", which was exactly what he wasn't, but I set out to make him love me.

Meo was a dear little thing and I felt sorry for him – he'd been so tiny when his mother, Camilla, had died.

But I couldn't help but think his mother must have been a nice woman, because Meo had the sweetest nature and I soon learned that he couldn't have inherited that from my husband.

My six younger brothers and sisters meant I was used to small children, so I knew how to play with Meo. I knew how to sing him songs and tell him stories, how to comfort him when he fell and grazed his knee and cuddle him when he was sad.

Meo was clever too, and I began to teach him his letters. I could see that Francesco was proud of his son, and pleased with me for taking such an interest in him.

It was the one thing in this house full of women that I could do, to love and care for this little boy. They expected it of me, but I surprised myself by how soon I came to think of Meo as my own son. And he called me Mamma just as quickly. I had a child without the dangers and terrors of giving birth.

EIGHT

Young Mother

But by the late summer after my wedding I was going to have a child of my own.

I first guessed when the smells from the kitchen turned my stomach and I could not eat anything except toasted bread. Then those weeks passed and before winter there was a definite bump under my dress.

Francesco was delighted and I was treated like a queen. I was protected from any upset or distress more than ever and given the best meats, the whitest bread, and the richest red wine.

My fear of childbirth grew with every month of my pregnancy, but I enjoyed all the fuss that was made of me. I was still only 16 and it was easy for me to push the thought of my coming ordeal to the back of my mind. Instead, I made the most of being the queen of the house.

Little Meo couldn't understand why there was less and less room for him to climb up on my lap. I told him, "You are going to be a big brother. Mamma has a new baby growing inside her. In a few more months the baby will be born."

The year turned and spring came. I had been married a year and now I felt less like "lovely Lisa" than ever. My belly was huge, my legs swollen and I could hardly walk. It was a relief when my mother moved in to help with the birth.

Francesco moved out of our room and slept in another. I was so restless, tossing and turning in our big bed at night, that he could get no peace. He worked so hard at his silk business that I felt guilty when I kept him awake.

When the pains started, my mother, Francesco's mother and all our sisters and sisters-in-law were there. But after many hours, I sent them away, apart from my mother and the midwife. They propped me up with pillows and supported me as I pushed.

I thought it would never end. But I was young and healthy and well-fed and so I brought little

Piero safely into the world. Later my mother told me that, in truth, it had not taken long for a first baby.

I was a month away from my 17th birthday and I had a son!

Francesco was so thrilled. Now he had two sons to carry on the family name and to follow him into the business. I had to smile when he said that. Francesco had mapped out the lives of a three-year-old and a tiny baby. But I knew it was only because he was so proud.

I lay back, exhausted, while Francesco took his new son to show off to his family. The midwife gently washed me and dressed me and put clean linen on my bed. Then she fed me chicken breast with extra salt and I drank some good wine and felt restored.

That night Francesco came into our room and kissed me and gave me a bracelet of rubies, to match his wedding gift of a pendant.

He slipped into bed beside me and put his arms tenderly around my sore body. "My lovely Lisa," he said, burying his face in my hair. "You have made me so happy."

Next morning, he took our baby to the Baptistery, with the godparents and many well-wishers. It was a bright sunny day in late May and I would have liked to go with them, but that was not our custom. And my legs still felt wobbly. Instead, the women lay me in a warm bath and I looked down at my naked body.

I was shocked to see that my belly was as big as it had been in the fifth month, but the midwife told me it would soon go down and I would be a slim young woman again.

My friends and kins-women all came to visit, with gifts for me and the baby. There were painted trays, which we would hang on our bedroom walls, and painted pottery dishes full of sweets, nuts and marzipan cakes.

Ginevra was one of my first visitors. She was married now and full of questions about what it had been like to bring a baby into the world.

"Not too hard," I said, as I didn't want to scare her. It would be her turn soon. "Not more than I could bear. And it was worth it – look at him!" The pains I had suffered were already fading in my memory.

The wet nurse had moved in with us as soon as little Piero was born. I had my son with me for only a week before the wet nurse took him into the countryside with her. It was our custom, but it made me sad to see my son in another woman's arms.

"Promise me we can visit him every week," I begged Francesco, unable to stop my tears. "I don't want Piero to grow up not knowing who his real mother is."

My husband hugged me and promised me that we would see our son as often as I liked.

After the baby left with his wet nurse my great comfort was Meo. He spent a lot of time cuddled up on my lap while I taught him his letters. It's the truth that I loved him just as much as I did little Piero. Meo's hugs and kisses helped me in that first year when Piero was away.

And by the time Piero came back home to me, I'd had another baby.

NINE

Always Crazy!

That year after Piero was born was terrible. I could no longer ignore the ravings of Savonarola, the mad preacher in the cathedral. I didn't go to hear him, but Francesco sometimes did. After the birth of Piero, I was expected to stay in the house for six weeks. Then it was summer and I spent some time in the country with Piero and Meo, while my husband stayed in Florence.

And when I came back it was not long before I was pregnant again.

But during this pregnancy I could hear the gangs of Savonarola's followers roaring around the streets near our house, singing songs that sounded at a distance like noisy, rude love songs.

It was only when they got closer and I could hear the words that I realised the songs were wild hymns about Our Lord. 'Crazy for Jesus' was the favourite, with its loud chorus of *"Crazy, always crazy, crazy, crazy!"*

I was terrified of these gangs and scared of bumping into them – so I stayed indoors more and more as the cold weather came.

And, when the year turned, as we got ready for Lent – the 40 days before Easter when we would eat no meat – Savonarola's gangs became bolder and started to knock on doors.

They wanted trinkets – lace, fans, jewels, combs, hair ornaments – everything not essential to life. Everything, you might say, that gave pleasure.

I knew that Savonarola had preached against these trinkets he called "vanities", but I wondered what he wanted them for. I had forgotten the old rumours.

It wasn't long until I found out.

We had given the gangs a few trinkets that no one would miss, but none of my best jewellery or lace. I took down Leonardo's sketch of me and hid it in my marriage chest. My husband got a new lock for our bedroom door, so there was no way the gangs could force their way in and take my treasures. These boys were becoming so bold that it seemed a real risk.

At the start of February, I couldn't stay indoors any longer. I decided to go for a walk, with a maid for company and protection.

It was a cold, crisp winter's day, with a promise of spring in the air. My heart lifted to be out on the streets of Florence again. I had got over my feelings of sickness with the new pregnancy and felt like a strong, healthy young woman again.

I loved all the festivities of Christmas, but it always cheered me to pass into the spring. In a few months I would have Piero back with me, which would ease the pain when I sent the new baby to the wet nurse.

We walked down the Via Larga and I remembered when I had walked up it on the day I moved to my husband's house nearly two years ago. We passed the cathedral and carried on down the long street of workshops that links Florence's two most important squares.

I was glad not to see Savonarola or any of his boys anywhere near the cathedral. We wandered past shops that my husband sold his silks to, and I was thinking about new fashions when we reached the Piazza della Signoria.

There, milling about in the square, were gangs of Savonarola's boys – the very people I wanted to avoid.

"What are they doing?" I whispered to the maid, as I clutched her arm in horror.

"They seem to be building something," she said and peered around me to look.

They were indeed building "something" and as we went closer, I could see what it was.

The boys were hurling all sorts of pretty things into a big heap in the square. I couldn't believe my eyes! I saw fans and feathered head-dresses and velvet slippers and paintings in gold frames and books bound in leather all being thrown on top of a stack of dry wood. It would go up in easy flames as soon as a light was set to it.

The boys had handcarts full of the things they had taken from the houses of Florence. There would be no Carnival this year – only fire and destruction.

I shrank back, aware of my calf-skin gloves and my velvet gown under my woollen cloak. Surely the boys wouldn't fall upon me and strip the luxuries from my body? But still I felt very afraid of these boys. They were so severe and yet pretended to be so pure and good.

"Let's go home," I told my maid and we turned and walked back the way we came as fast as we could.

At dinner, I told Francesco what I had seen.

He nodded, his face grim. "I know," he said. "I've seen it. They will set fire to it all on Tuesday. And, until then, there will be a guard in case anyone comes to take things off the bonfire."

"Tuesday!" I cried. "So instead of our Carnival of Shrove Tuesday there will be a horrid fire to burn the pretty treasures of the young women of Florence."

"*Ssh*. You mustn't get upset," Francesco's mother said. "It *is* horrid, but what can we do as long as Savonarola is the ruler of our city?"

"I wish the Medici were back," I said, and I felt my tears about to fall. "I wish Lorenzo hadn't died. I hate the way life is in the city now."

"There are many people who feel as you do," Francesco said. "And together with those who support Savonarola, this whole city is as ready to burst into flames as that awful bonfire."

That night I couldn't sleep and when I did, I had nightmares. I saw Leonardo's sketch of me as a little child as it curled up and blackened in the fierce flames of the bonfire.

TEN

One Small Flaw

Florence was no longer a good place to live.

I had no more nightmares but I could feel the tension in the air. Francesco told me that the bonfire had been lit and all the "vanities" had been burned. It was meant as a sign that the city must repent. People, especially women, should dress in a sober way and stop decorating their faces and bodies with make-up and jewels.

I had never thought myself vain, but I had always been so praised for my beauty that it was hard for me to believe there was anything wrong in wanting to look my best.

In my heart I didn't think it would happen, but I worried for my husband's business if the women of Florence stopped wearing silks and other rich fabrics.

"Savonarola has fallen out with Pope Alexander now," my husband told me. "The Pope is tired of the rumours the preacher keeps spreading about him."

I didn't know too much about religion or politics, but I guessed that when Savonarola said the Pope was corrupt, he might have been right. Even I had heard that Pope Alexander had several children by different women.

"Do you think the Pope will get rid of him?" I asked.

"He certainly wants to," Francesco said, his face grim. "We must wait and see."

I was in the last month of my pregnancy and starting to withdraw from the world, when we heard some news. The Pope had excommunicated Savonarola – which meant the preacher could no longer take Communion or perform the Mass.

This was the most severe punishment, apart from death. To be cut off like this was intended as a great blow. But Savonarola just ignored the Pope and carried on as normal.

And my time was coming and I had things nearer to home to busy myself with.

Childbirth was easier this time because I knew what to expect and my body had done it before. My sweet daughter Piera came into the world a year after her brother, without any difficulty.

I was so pleased it was a girl this time. We named her after Francesco's mother, which pleased her very much. My mother and I had not always got on well, but I hoped for a good and loving relationship with my daughter. And, from the start, Francesco doted on his first daughter.

Again, I had to let my child go, to a wet nurse in the country, but the same wet nurse brought my Piero back to me and that was a great comfort. Piero hadn't forgotten that I was his mother and was as loving as his brother Meo. I felt that Francesco and I had almost forgotten Meo had another mother at his birth. He was as much ours as little Piero.

And now I had a daughter to go with my sons, who would return to me well-fed and healthy.

I felt blessed.

*

I only rarely thought about Leonardo, the angelic painter. I got the odd bit of news from my father, who was still friends with Piero, Leonardo's father. He told me that Leonardo was doing great things in Milan. There were rumours of a wonderful wall-painting that showed Our Lord at his last meal with his disciples.

I longed to see it, but I had never travelled further from my home city than the countryside around it. I was not likely to go so far now, with my growing family.

In fact, I had now lost all contact with artists, as my friend Michelangelo had left Florence too, before I was married. I think Michelangelo was in Rome at this time, and no one knew when or if he would return.

I had no idea what part Michelangelo and Leonardo, these two great artists, would still play in the life of Florence – and in my life too.

The only small cloud in my happiness was my husband's temper. I learned that I had married a bad-tempered man.

Oh, Francesco never showed his temper to me. He was always kind. But remember how many members of his family lived in the house with us? It was a big house, but I still overheard his quarrels with his brothers and these seemed to happen more and more.

He would complain to me of customers who were slow to pay, of suppliers who demanded their money in advance. I could hear in his voice how angrily he must have spoken to them.

This temper was the only flaw in a good man and I tried not to think about it too much. Francesco was always loving to me and I knew it could have been much worse.

But I didn't want his children to grow up with the same flaw and I watched them for any signs of bad temper.

ELEVEN

Sunshine and Tears

Before Piera was a year old, Savonarola was no more.

The start of Lent was a few weeks later that year, almost at the end of February. And it was marked with another bonfire, piled high with the trinkets that made the women of Florence happy. But in March the tide turned against Savonarola and he stopped preaching.

Then he went a bit mad – or madder – and ranted about how he could perform miracles. So, at the start of April, there was to be another fire in the Piazza della Signoria. This was a trial by fire. Two men were to walk through fire to prove who was right, Savonarola or his opponents.

But in the end there was no trial and no miracle, because the rain poured down and put the fire out.

People blamed Savonarola for the disaster. Huge crowds had gathered in the Piazza to see the "miracle" and they were disappointed, and cold and wet too. It wasn't long before Savonarola was arrested and his hold over Florence was at an end.

He was tortured over and over again and then condemned to death. Much as I was terrified of Savonarola and hated his contempt for women and their pleasures, I was shocked by what happened to him.

Again, a fire was lit in the Piazza, but not to burn "vanities" or produce "miracles".

I didn't go to the execution, but my husband did, along with most of the men in Florence. Two other preachers were to hang with Savonarola and then all three bodies would be burned. The ashes would be flung in the river, so the preacher's crazy followers couldn't keep them as holy relics.

"They had to carry Savonarola to the scaffold," Francesco told me. "He was so broken by the torture that he couldn't stand."

"And were they all hanged and burned?" I asked.

My husband nodded.

"There is nothing left of them," he said. "I don't know about the other two men, but Florence is well rid of Savonarola. We can all breathe easier now he has gone."

I knew Francesco hoped his business would do better now that customers didn't have to worry that their fine silks might be thrown on to a bonfire.

But I said a prayer for Savonarola and the two other preachers that night. After all, they were human beings, even if Savonarola had been so harsh and cruel. The preacher had warned of the pains of hell fire and I wondered if he was feeling them now.

*

Soon I had pains of my own to bear.

I had only a year with my first daughter, after she came back from the wet nurse. Dear little Piera lived only two years in this world. When we lost her I didn't know how to carry on. I had never felt grief so sharp or so deep.

But what could I do? I still had Meo and Piero and I was very pregnant with my third child. I gave birth to a second daughter, Camilla, just a few months after we lost Piera. It was lovely to hold another baby girl in my arms, but little Camilla could not replace her lost sister.

I spent months crying or trying not to cry. I felt as if I would never smile again.

In time the pain eased. Piera's death made me worry about the health of the three children I had, including Meo, who was now a sturdy five-year-old. But I had to accept that the death of a child happened often to parents.

Babies died in the womb or at birth, often taking their mothers with them. Or children didn't live to see their 10th birthdays.

Ginevra lost her first child with Bernardo, but now had a fine one-year-old boy, Tommaso. Ginevra was so kind to me when we lost Piera, and came to sit with me day after day, while her son was away being nursed. It was good that she didn't have Tommaso with her. I felt so tender that I didn't want to see anyone else's baby.

Ginevra understood all I felt, having lost a child herself.

And she brought me news of the outside world. In my grief, I had not kept up with life in Florence, let alone life outside its city walls.

But that summer a French army had invaded Milan. I was interested in spite of my heavy heart. Leonardo was still at the court of the Duke of Milan – and I wondered what this would mean for him.

Was he safe? Would he come back to Florence? Would I see him again?

Ginevra wouldn't have been able to answer those questions even if I had asked them out loud. But somehow I was sure that Leonardo would head home.

By the time I felt able to go to church, I saw another face from the past.

Michelangelo was back from Rome. He took my hand and told me I looked thin and pale.

"What has happened to you since I left Florence?" he asked.

"Too much to tell in a few words," I said, as I tried to hold back my tears. "Marriage, motherhood, gains and losses."

Michelangelo looked intensely at my face.

"I hope you are happy," he said. "At least, I hope you will be happy again when you have recovered from whatever has made you sad."

This was a long speech for my childhood friend and I knew he meant it.

"I want to see you smile again," he said gently.

I looked at him and, for the first time, I thought perhaps I might.

TWELVE

Starting Again

In Florence we celebrate the start of a new year in March, on the day the angel sent a message to Our Lady that she was to bear a divine child. And that March marked the start not just of a new year but of a new century.

I pulled myself together. This was a good moment to start my life afresh. One thing I knew was that the year 1500 would bring another child for me. This was what I expected from marriage – a new baby every year or two and a family of five or six children.

Women of my social class took this for granted, just as they knew that out of every six babies born, one or two might never grow up. Very rarely, there was a couple who seemed unable to have any children at all and then we felt so sorry for them, especially for the wife. I was relieved that I wasn't one of those sad women, but no one ever knew whether they would be able to have a family until they were married.

So I was going to have a fourth baby and had already lost one. I'd be 21 that summer. By anyone's standards I was an adult woman.

And yet the rumour that filled the city soon after the new year set my heart a-flutter, as if I had still been a 15-year-old romantic girl again.

Leonardo was on his way back!

His reputation was such that all of Florence was keen to see him again. He might have been born in Vinci, but he was regarded as a true Florentine. Hadn't he grown up here and wasn't his father living in the Via Ghibellina?

Old Piero da Vinci was on to his fourth wife now and had eleven more children, the youngest just a toddler. His oldest son, Leonardo, at nearly 48, wouldn't lodge with all the others in that crowded house, would he?

No. Leonardo would stay as an honoured guest at the church of the Most Holy

Annunciation, where we had all celebrated the new year.

I couldn't wait to see Leonardo again, even though I could hardly remember him. Still, he couldn't have changed as much as I had in the last 18 years.

Michelangelo was the only person I knew who wasn't excited about the artist's return to our city. I made the mistake of mentioning it to him after church one Sunday.

"We shall soon see if he's such a great artist," Michelangelo growled at me. "I hear that the *Last Supper* he painted in Milan is already falling off the wall. And he was never able to cast that bronze statue of the duke on horseback. I don't think he deserves his great reputation."

Michelangelo was jealous! He was the younger man by 25 years, but instead of respecting the older artist, he saw him as a rival. He couldn't wait to topple Leonardo off the high place he held in people's minds.

But I bit my tongue and turned our talk to more pleasant matters.

"I heard your own reputation was very high in Rome before you came back," I said.

Michelangelo grunted, but I could see he was pleased.

"It's true that people seem to like my sculptures," he said.

"I wish I could see them," I said. "But I have never travelled far outside Florence."

"You won't have to travel to see my next statue," he said. "Not if I get the work I'm after."

"You are going to make a statue here in Florence?" I asked, but he wouldn't say any more.

*

One day I was visiting Francesco in his workshop when a distinguished man came in. He was of late middle age, his long hair more silver than gold, but he was still handsome. You could see he was a person of importance.

A lovely scent of violets hovered around him and he was followed by a group of young men, who seemed to be his students or his admirers.

I knew him straight away.

But he didn't know me. How could he?

Leonardo had last seen me as a three-year-old child and I was now a wife and mother, expecting another baby.

"May I present my wife?" Francesco said. "Lisa Gherardini. Lisa, this is the great painter come back to us – Leonardo, Ser da Vinci's oldest son."

It wasn't till he heard my name that recognition dawned. Leonardo took my hand and kissed it.

"The pretty baby!" he said, with a smile. "I knew you would become a great beauty and I was right. Francesco del Giocondo, you have won a fine prize."

I blushed like a girl at this praise. I wondered if Leonardo spoke to all women in this way or if I was as special to him as he was to me. He had no idea how often I had thought about him when he was away.

And here he was, holding on to my hand and gazing into my eyes as if searching for something in my face.

"Yes," he said at last, and let go of my hand. "I *can* see traces of that lovely Lisa, who was just a child when I left Florence."

He turned to Francesco. "It makes me feel old," he said. "I have been away too long if that pretty child is now a wife and mother."

Then Leonardo asked after my parents and wanted to know of our children. He seemed truly interested.

Not so the knot of young men who had come into the workshop after him. They lounged about in a bored way, sometimes feeling a bolt of silk between their fingers and talking together in whispers.

"I hope you will let me call on you, Monna Lisa," Leonardo said as he left the workshop. "It would be a pleasure to see your father again too."

Then he was gone, leaving only that lovely scent of violets.

THIRTEEN
The Rivals

Well, Leonardo did call on us and I was proud to be dressed in my finest clothes and for the artist to see me in such a grand house.

Leonardo came on his own, without his knot of young men, but Francesco told me he was rarely seen about town without them.

"You know the rumours?" Francesco said. "He is a great painter and I am honoured to know him, but you know what he was accused of in 1476?"

"That was before I was born," I said. "Was he convicted?"

"No," Francesco admitted. "But Leonardo left Florence and no one knew where he went. I was only a lad, but as soon as I knew anything about him I knew that he, er, was unlikely to marry. That he liked boys. Do you understand?"

Of course I did! Everyone knew that there were different rules for men and women. And that many men in Florence had experiences with other men as well as women before they wed. Their wives, on the other hand, had to be pure. Perhaps that's why we women became wives so young – before we'd had a chance to be naughty!

Still, some men stuck to their preference for other men and it seemed that Leonardo was one of them.

I nodded to Francesco and smiled, and we didn't speak of it again.

It wasn't long before my third daughter was born, by which time Leonardo had left the city again. Little Marietta was another comfort to me and, just as she left with her wet nurse, my Camilla came back, so I had a daughter with me to love.

I sensed that Francesco had hoped for a boy this time, but he was too polite to say anything and gave me a string of glowing pearls when Marietta was born. He had been almost as upset as I was when our little Piera died, and I saw that our two girls were a comfort to him too. After all, he had Meo and Piero, so he wasn't without sons.

I soon recovered from the birth and went back to church where I saw my old friend Michelangelo. And now all Florence knew what he had meant when he told me I should see his next statue.

He had been commissioned to carve a David out of a block of Carrara marble that had been lying about for over 40 years. Two other sculptors had tried and failed to carve anything from the beautiful, pure white stone.

"They said it had a flaw in it," Michelangelo told me and Francesco. "But the flaw was in them. They couldn't see what I can in that block."

Even on a Sunday his clothes were covered in dust from chiselling away at the marble and for the next few years he was totally absorbed in that giant block.

In the meantime, Leonardo was supposed to be working on a huge altarpiece for the church of the Most Holy Annunciation. But I had heard talk that his progress was slow.

So, while Michelangelo worked in a hail of marble chips, Leonardo spent a lot of time in fashionable places, wearing elegant clothes and with his group of young men always close by.

But Leonardo must have been thinking about the altarpiece, too. We all heard that he was going to exhibit the drawing his work would be based on in the church.

And so every citizen in Florence came to that room at the church where Leonardo's drawing was on display.

The drawing was huge and the figures gigantic – the Virgin Mary and her mother Saint Anne. Even the baby Jesus and the child Saint John seemed larger than life. There was no doubt this painting would be a masterpiece.

My husband and I were there at the same time as Michelangelo, who studied the drawing for a long time with an artist's eye.

At last, Michelangelo gave a grunt and a nod, as if to admit to Leonardo's talent, and then he left the church. Leonardo had been looking on, amused, the whole time.

"He's such a bear, isn't he, young Michelangelo?" Leonardo said to Francesco. "But a great artist, so we must put up with his ways."

"I don't see why," Francesco said. "You are a great artist and yet you behave like a gentleman."

Leonardo laughed.

"Come back and dine with us," my husband said. "When everyone has left."

I hoped Leonardo would visit us on his own, without his group of young men.

There was one in particular that I didn't like. They called him "*Salai*" or "little devil" and I could see why. He had been in Leonardo's household since he was a boy, but was about 22 now and very jealous about his master.

"You wouldn't believe what he was like at ten," Leonardo told me that evening, when Salai was not around. "He was a greedy, lying little thief, with an appetite as big as five men's. But I have at last tamed him."

I wasn't at all sure he had.

FOURTEEN

War and Peace

One day we heard that Leonardo had disappeared. And then came the rumour that he had gone to serve Duke Cesare Borgia in Urbino. It was like saying Leonardo had gone to work for the Devil himself, such was the fear everyone in Florence had for the brutal duke.

I was sad to think Leonardo had left without a goodbye, but I was expecting another baby and I had other things to think about too.

Florence was enjoying a period of calm, after the death of Savonarola. For four years now the city had been governed as a Republic by Piero Soderini and I was no longer nervous about wearing silk dresses and lace. But there were still some of Savonarola's supporters who were angry about his death. They were the enemies of those who wanted to bring back the Medici family from exile.

Ginevra was pregnant too and we spent a lot of time together, talking about husbands and children. We laughed at how long ago it was since we had been carefree girls with our dreams of the handsome Giuliano de' Medici. But we were happy.

Not so my husband. Francesco seemed always to be arguing these days – with customers, with suppliers, with his brothers, with the servants. His temper, always short, was now bursting out into angry words and violent acts.

It was still the only cloud on my horizon. I had all my children home with me – Piero, Camilla and Marietta, a new baby on the way, and Meo now a big boy of nine, who was as loving to me as he had always been.

When I got ready to give birth, I had the fears of all women about the health of my new-born. But Camilla and Marietta were already older than little Piera had been when she died, so I tried to believe that all the omens were good.

I was rewarded by the arrival of my second son, Andrea, in December. Much as I loved all my daughters, it was wonderful to see how excited Francesco was at the birth of his third son. He felt so confident now that his business was safe for the next generation that his harsh temper became softer.

He gave me another magnificent gift – a necklace of moonstones, the gem of my birth month. I was just happy to have made my husband so glad.

And in the spring he did something that made me even happier – he bought the house next door!

"I am tired of falling over my brothers and their families," he said. "It's time we had a home of our own."

I couldn't believe it! A house for the two of us, our children and some servants was going to be the greatest luxury I had ever known. But moving – even if it was only next door – kept me busy for weeks. Everything had to be selected and packed with care, servants had to be chosen to come with us or new ones hired. And I had not long come out of my six weeks of confinement after Andrea's birth.

But all the busyness kept my mind off the loss of my new baby to his wet nurse. I was used to that by now and knew the year would pass swiftly till he came back to me.

The new house was a much happier home. I don't just mean the Persian rugs on the wooden floors or the leaded glass in the windows that flooded the house with spring sunshine. We had space – I hadn't realised how crowded the old family house had become.

Francesco's temper softened some more and a wonderful sense of peace spread over the house. It wasn't always quiet, with four young children, but they were all our own. The noisy chaos of nephews and nieces on top of one another had been left behind.

My marriage chest stood at the foot of our bed and the precious sketch by Leonardo had found its proper place on the wall of our new room.

As he looked at it one night, Francesco said, "Do you know what I would like? A proper portrait of you as you are now."

"Painted by Leonardo I suppose," I said, to tease him. I was feeling very fond of my husband.

"Why not?" he asked.

"Well, because he is the most famous painter in Italy, maybe in Europe," I said. "And isn't he still building engines of war for Cesare Borgia?"

"Not any more," Francesco said. "I bumped into him in the street today, as a matter of fact. He is back in Florence."

This news took my breath away. My younger self would have longed to spend hours alone with the painter. But my older self just wanted to see what he would make of my face today.

"Won't it be dreadfully expensive?" I asked.

Francesco flung out one arm in a generous gesture. "Nothing is too expensive for my wife, the mother of my children," he said. "That's settled. I will ask Leonardo tomorrow. And when it is finished it will hang in our *salone* and people will come from all over Italy to look at the wonder that is my lovely Lisa!"

I had thought myself lucky to have a rich husband, healthy children and a handsome new home. And now I was to have my portrait painted by the great Leonardo. Perhaps I would even become famous.

And then I heard one of the children howl and I put such foolish dreams out of my head. After all, I was nothing more than the wife of a silk merchant.

FIFTEEN

Monna Lisa

When Francesco got an idea into his head, he was like a dog with a bone. So it wasn't long before he came home one day with a big grin and some welcome news.

"Leonardo has agreed to paint your portrait, Lisa," Francesco said, and he took both my hands in his. "He is coming here tomorrow to start the sketches!"

"Tomorrow?"

All I could think of was what I should wear and whether the right clothes would be clean and ready in time. I spent the evening taking every garment I owned out of its chest and upsetting the servants.

All for nothing. The next day Leonardo soon showed me how foolish I had been.

I greeted him in the full glory of my bridal clothes, which I was proud I could still wear un-altered after five children. My ruby pendant was about my neck, my ruby bracelet on my wrist, and my hands were heavy with rings.

"You are magnificent today, Monna Lisa," Leonardo said. He bent to plant a kiss on my hand where he could find a space amid the gold and jewels.

"But you do me too much honour," he went on. "Today I shall draw only your face, as I did when you were a smiling baby, and all this finery will not be seen."

I blushed like a silly girl showing off, rather than a wife and mother who ran her own household. But I pulled myself together and decided to dress more simply the next time.

Still it was not simple enough for Maestro Leonardo!

This next time I had gone with my maid to Leonardo's studio in Santa Maria Novella.

"I want you to sit like this," he told me, and he sat me on a chair so that I was half turned towards him. "I will paint the background later. But I want you to wear your simplest, darkest dress and no ornament or jewels except perhaps a Spanish veil."

I was sorry that this picture, to be hung on our *salone* wall, would show me looking so plain. But then anyone who saw it would also see me – in real life – and I could dress in my finery by contrast. That idea cheered me up.

I didn't go to Leonardo's studio every day. My household duties and his other work made that impossible. But whenever he sent a note that he would be available, I made time to visit.

My only problem was that Salai was almost always there for our sittings. He was like a fly buzzing in the window that you can't get out of the room or swat.

I could see that Salai must have been very handsome as a boy, but he was now losing his looks. He was still young of course – about the same age as me – but I feared his greed and lack of self-control had aged him before his time.

Still, Leonardo seemed fond of Salai and able to keep him in check, so I put up with him as best I could.

And there were other distractions. It was Leonardo's idea that I should not be bored while I sat for him and so it was Salai's task to organise musicians to entertain me.

"I want to paint you smiling," Leonardo said. "Your smile is all the ornament you need."

I was flattered and I soon began to relax.

I didn't need the music – Leonardo's talk kept me amused. He had travelled to so many places and seen so many people and things – dukes, court life, battles, engines of war. He told me about Milan, a city I had never visited, and how well he had been treated there before the French army invaded and he had to flee.

Salai lounged around in the studio, but Leonardo would often send him out on errands. I was always more comfortable when he had gone and I think Leonardo sensed that.

One day I found Leonardo had added columns to the painting on either side of me and had started to sketch in a distant landscape behind me. I stopped looking at the painting as my portrait and realised how remarkable it was. I wondered how it would feel to see it on a wall in my home.

SIXTEEN
Two Masterpieces

In the summer of 1503, my husband and I were invited to the public showing of Michelangelo's statue, which everyone called "The Giant". It wasn't quite finished – we had to view it in his workshop behind the cathedral – but it was the biggest sensation in our city since Leonardo's drawing in the church of the Most Holy Annunciation.

Francesco and I met many friends at the showing, and we were all in awe. Michelangelo's statue was indeed massive, but the carving was very light and delicate.

I blushed when I realised this larger than life and very handsome "man" was totally naked, but I soon became absorbed in looking at his face. He was the shepherd boy David from the Bible, the one who went on to be King of the Israelites. But this statue showed him from earlier in his story, when, armed only with a slingshot, he fought a real giant called Goliath.

It was a popular story in Florence as it represented the Republic – the small person up against the strength of great armies. Florence already had many images of the young David – by the famous Donatello and by Verrocchio, who taught Leonardo. Some people thought Leonardo had been the model for his master's bronze David.

But Michelangelo had done something very different. Not only was his statue naked and gigantic, his David hadn't killed Goliath yet. There was no severed head at his feet. This David was about to throw the stone that felled Goliath. We knew David would be the winner, but he didn't.

It was a masterpiece.

The only friend who didn't come to see it was Leonardo, who had been called to Pisa on a secret mission. I thought how he was a mystery – much more than "just" a painter. Who knew what Leonardo was involved in now?

But everyone in Florence was talking about the Giant. It made Salai jealous on Leonardo's behalf. And someone began a rumour that another masterpiece was being created in Florence at the same time. When Leonardo returned from Pisa, people started calling at his studio to look at his painting of me!

Rumours flew that Leonardo was painting his best picture and for a while he basked in the glory of people admiring his genius.

These visitors gave Salai a role that suited him. Whenever I went to Leonardo's studio, I found him offering visitors wine and cake, entertaining them with his stories. Some even stayed while Leonardo painted me. I was far more embarrassed than Leonardo, who was very relaxed about people watching him as he worked. I, on the other hand, felt very ill at ease as others gazed at my face.

I thought about Michelangelo and how he had carved his great statue in private – almost in secret – with a wall around him and a roof above his head. The two artists couldn't have been more different. That public showing of his David, ordered by the Signoria, must have been agony for Michelangelo.

By the autumn I could see my face emerging from the background of Leonardo's portrait. I didn't know whether to feel flattered or disappointed.

The woman who looked back at me was not as beautiful as I hoped I was, but I hadn't spent much time looking in mirrors these last few years. As I looked longer at her, I could see Leonardo had given me something that was more than beauty, but I couldn't put a name to it.

Leonardo watched me with a little smile as I looked at his work.

"Does it please you, Monna Lisa?" he asked.

"It does," I said, after some time, and I let myself smile.

"That is what I have tried to capture!" he said, and he brushed my mouth with the tips of his fingers.

But still something made me uneasy. That night I woke with a start when at last I realised what it was.

Something in the portrait's face reminded me not of myself, but of Salai.

*

Soon after, Leonardo got another commission and our sittings stopped for a time.

The Republic of Florence had decided he should paint a mural in a grand new room in the Palazzo della Signoria. It was to depict a battle – not Leonardo's usual subject. But the commission was an honour and I couldn't complain that his focus was now on that instead of on painting an ordinary housewife.

Francesco didn't see it that way. "If our friend Leonardo has a flaw," he said when he heard I hadn't been to the studio for over a month, "it is that he tends not to finish what he starts. I can't wait to have your likeness up on that wall. And think what a treasure we will leave to our children!"

"But he can hardly refuse such an important piece of work for the Signoria," I said, as I wondered what Francesco would do if Leonardo didn't finish my portrait.

"True, but we must keep him up to the mark."

Then it was December and my little Andrea came back from the country and I was content. I had all my children about me and the woman in the portrait seemed like another person. She led her silent, smiling life in a painting on an easel in a great man's studio while he sketched out a much grander design.

SEVENTEEN

Departures

The year turned again and with the new one came losses. Leonardo's father, old Piero, died at nearly 80 years old. The painter was upset, but even more so when he found that his father had left him nothing. All Piero's estate went to his nine lawful sons and two lawful daughters. It was a slap in the face for Leonardo, his oldest child, forever excluded from his father's full love.

I couldn't understand it. If my Piero or Andrea – or Meo – had shown even a tenth of Leonardo's talents, I would have burst with pride. I couldn't imagine having a son born out of wedlock, of course, but I hoped that would not have stopped me loving him fully.

Then Leonardo took another blow.

The Signoria commissioned Michelangelo to paint another mural in their grand new room, on the wall opposite the one Leonardo was working on. It was to be another battle, so everyone in Florence soon called it the "Battle of the Battles". We all knew the Signoria was taking advantage of Leonardo's rivalry with Michelangelo, and it was really the "Battle of the Artists".

Leonardo was now over 50 years old, and felt insulted to have this young man of not yet 30 pitted against him. But unlike my hot-headed friend Michelangelo, Leonardo was always polite and well-mannered, so he kept his anger to himself.

But almost as soon as he'd heard about the second commission for Michelangelo, Leonardo left for Milan. And I began to think, like Francesco, that my portrait might never be finished.

Leonardo did come back and he did continue to work on his battle mural in the Palazzo della Signoria. But very soon after that it went wrong – the paint ran. Leonardo was furious and said he had been sold cheap oil to mix his colours with.

But then it was Michelangelo's turn to leave Florence, for Rome. No one knew it then, but he was to spend most of the rest of his life in the Holy City. Michelangelo's mural to rival Leonardo's never got further than a sketch or two.

It seemed that my brief spell as the muse of a great artist was well and truly over, and so I put the painting out of my mind and focused on the things I knew – caring for my children and running a comfortable home for my husband.

Much to my surprise, five years after little Andrea was born, I was pregnant again and a third son was given to us. Alas for too short a time. Giocondo slipped away after just a month and I was even more stricken by grief than when we lost Piera. We had had Piera for two years, but Giocondo stayed only a few weeks. I was ill, weepy and sad.

Leonardo came to pay his respects and it was at a time when Francesco was away on business. My husband hadn't wanted to leave me, but it was urgent and I told him he must go.

Even the sight of the painter and the warmth of his greetings couldn't lift my spirits. And then he made it so much worse.

"I've come to tell you I am leaving, Monna Lisa," Leonardo said.

"Leaving Florence?"

"Leaving Italy," he said. "I am going to the court of the French king."

At that moment, I saw my life stretch out in front of me with no more art or beauty or colour left in it. A tear fell on my black silk dress. Leonardo took my hand.

"I shall take you with me," he said.

I shook my head, unable to believe my ears.

"Your likeness, I mean," Leonardo went on. "I will take your portrait to France with me and work on it."

"Does it need much more work?" I asked, as I gathered my wits. "It looked almost finished when I last saw it."

"I think it could be even better," he said.

We were silent for a while. Then I said, "Can I ask you something? Why do you make me look like Salai?"

Leonardo looked startled. "You do have a look of him when you smile," he said. He still held my hand as he said in a soft voice, "The life you have is what I can never have – marriage, sweet children, contentment in your own home. But I do know love."

"Francesco will be disappointed not to have the portrait," I said.

"He has something much finer," said Leonardo. "He has the original."

We sat in silence a little longer and my heart was full of what might have been.

"Lisa," Leonardo said, his voice tender. "You know you will not always be sad. You have had a terrible loss but you are young and have so much to live for."

"I know," I said. "I know I am lucky, but it hurts so much to lose a child."

"I can only imagine," he said. "But I don't want to leave you while you are sad. Will you promise me that one day you will smile again? I don't want to feel I am taking your smile to France and leaving you here to weep."

I tried, I really did, but that smile came out as a very shaky, wobbly one.

Leonardo took out a piece of paper and some red chalk from the leather bag he always had with him. Quickly, he sketched my face and showed me what he had done.

A sad face looked back at me. Then he rubbed out the mouth and re-drew it into a gentle smile. He handed me my new portrait and I couldn't help it. I smiled back at the woman smiling up at me.

"Thank you," I said.

"Keep it," he said, and he pointed at the wall behind me. "Put it up on your wall until I bring you back your portrait in oils. It will remind you of a time when you were happy."

"It will remind me of you," I said.

"Goodbye, lovely Lisa," Leonardo said, as he got up to leave. "I promise to bring you your portrait when it is finished."

When he had gone, I sat with the red chalk drawing in my lap and I didn't cry any more for fear I would spoil it with my tears.

And then Francesco was in the room. Ever the kind husband, he had come back early from his business trip to be with me.

He found me sitting in the dark and called for a servant to light the lamps.

"What's this, Lisa?" he asked. "Has Leonardo been here? Why are you in the dark?"

I pulled myself together.

"Yes, but he is leaving Italy for France," I said.

"What about your portrait?" my husband said, as I knew he would.

"He promises to bring it back as soon as it is finished," I said. But even as I spoke, I knew that the portrait would never be finished and I would never see it again.

Francesco shrugged. "Let's have the children in," he said. "I've brought back presents for them."

"Yes, let's," I said. And I smiled.

A Note on *Smile*

There have been many theories about the woman who posed for Leonardo da Vinci's portrait known as the *Mona Lisa*, now in the Musée du Louvre in Paris.

I believe that the most likely model is Lisa Gherardini, the wife of a Florentine silk merchant called Francesco del Giocondo. The painting is sometimes called *La Gioconda*, which could mean "wife of Giocondo" or "the happy one", which fits well with the portrait's famous smile.

Leonardo never handed over his painting to Francesco del Giocondo. He still had it when he died in France in 1519, more than ten years after he left Florence. It must have had some deep personal meaning for him.

I have made the story of *Smile* up, apart from the facts of births, deaths and marriages. I have invented Leonardo's earlier sketches of the child "Lovely Lisa" and Lisa's stormy relationship with her mother.

Mary Hoffman
Summer, 2017

Our books are tested
for children and young people by
children and young people.

Thanks to everyone who consulted on
a manuscript for their time and effort in
helping us to make our books better
for our readers.